STAR WARS®

THE CLONE WARS™

SLAVES OF THE REPUBLIC
VOLUME SIX
"ESCAPE FROM KADAVO"

SCRIPT
HENRY GILROY

PENCILS
SCOTT HEPBURN

INKS
DAN PARSONS

COLORS
MICHAEL E. WIGGAM

LETTERING
MICHAEL HEISLER

COVER ART
LE TANG

Jedi Knights Anakin and Obi-Wan, along with Ahsoka and Captain Rex, have at long last located the missing Togruta people of the Kiros colony. Posing as slavers, the Jedi have infiltrated the Zygerrian homeworld to attend an auction, where the slavers mean to sell the eight million souls to the highest bidder.

At the auction the Jedi are discovered, captured by the Zygerrian queen, and forced into slavery themselves. To keep his friends alive, Anakin becomes the queen's bodyguard, and she soon develops feelings for him. Refusing to allow Anakin to be executed by Count Dooku, the queen pays with her life.

Having escaped and freed Ahsoka, Anakin races across the galaxy to rescue Obi-Wan, Captain Rex, and the Togruta who have been imprisoned in a slave-processing facility, where their will is to be broken . . .

DARK HORSE COMICS

Spotlight

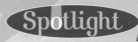

VISIT US AT
www.abdopublishing.com

Reinforced library bound edition published in 2010 by Spotlight, a division of the ABDO Group, 8000 West 78th Street, Edina, Minnesota 55439. Spotlight produces high-quality reinforced library bound editions for schools and libraries. Published by agreement with Dark Horse Comics, Inc., and Lucasfilm Ltd.

Printed in the United States of America, Melrose Park, Illinois.
092009
012010

 PRINTED ON RECYCLED PAPER

Library of Congress Cataloging-in-Publication Data

Gilroy, Henry.
  Slaves of the republic / script by Henry Gilroy ; pencils by Scott Hepburn ; inks by Dan Parsons ; colors by Michael E. Wiggam ; lettering by Michael Heisler.
-- Reinforced library bound ed.
    v. cm. -- (Star wars: the clone wars)
  "Dark Horse Comics."
  Contents: v. 1. The mystery of Kiros -- v. 2. Slave traders of Zygerria -- v. 3. The depths of Zygerria -- v. 4. Auction of a million souls -- v. 5. A slave now, a slave forever -- v. 6. Escape from kadavo.
  ISBN 978-1-59961-710-7 (v. 1) -- ISBN 978-1-59961-711-4 (v. 2) -- ISBN 978-1-59961-712-1 (v. 3) -- ISBN 978-1-59961-713-8 (v. 4) -- ISBN 978-1-59961-714-5 (v. 5) -- ISBN 978-1-59961-715-2 (v. 6)
  1. Graphic novels. [1. Graphic novels.] I. Hepburn, Scott. II. Star Wars, the clone wars (Television program) III. Title.
  PZ7.7.G55Sl 2010
  [Fic]--dc22
                    2009030553

All Spotlight books have reinforced library bindings and are manufactured in the United States of America.

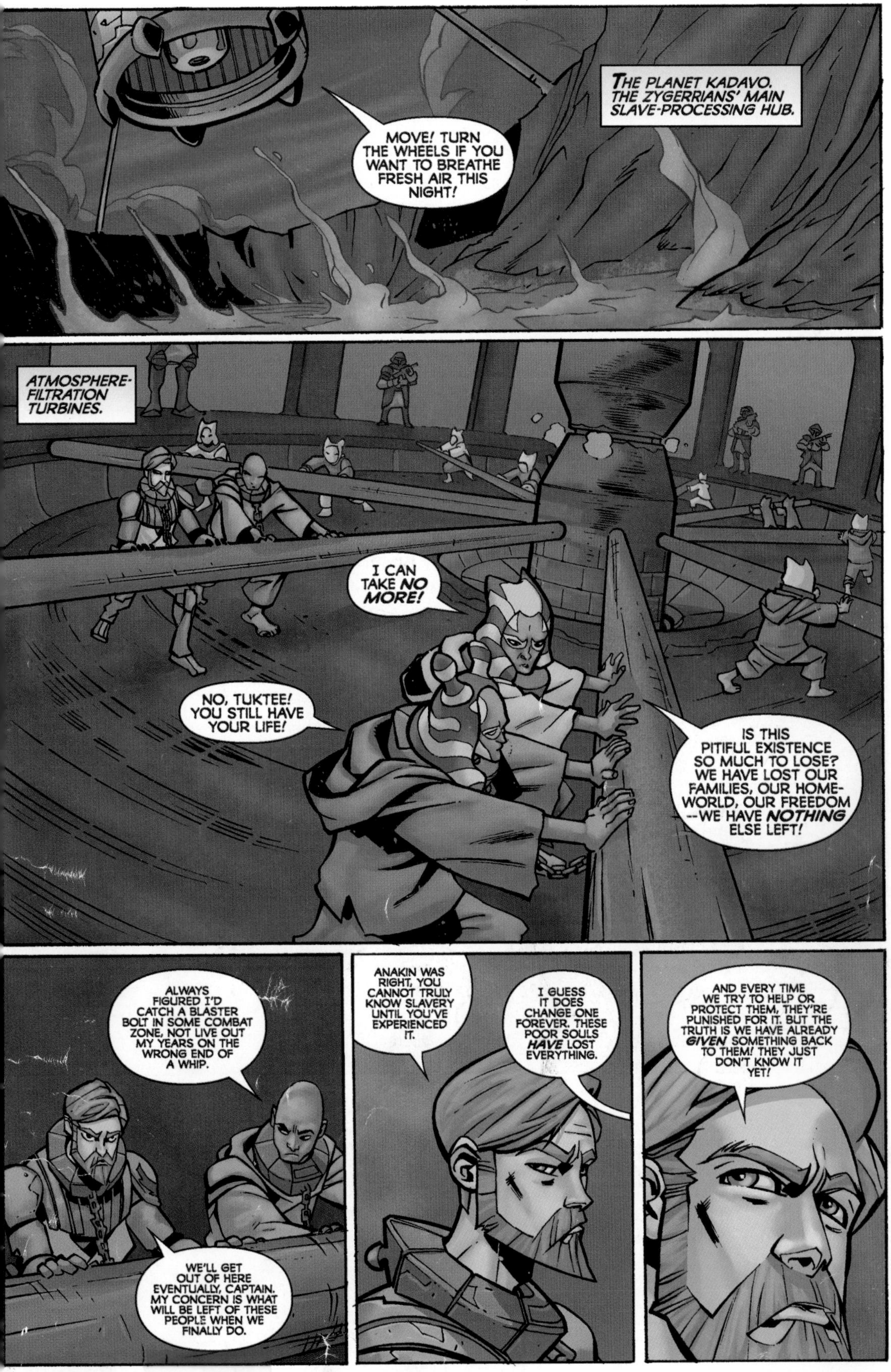
THE PLANET KADAVO. THE ZYGERRIANS' MAIN SLAVE-PROCESSING HUB.
MOVE! TURN THE WHEELS IF YOU WANT TO BREATHE FRESH AIR THIS NIGHT!
ATMOSPHERE-FILTRATION TURBINES.
I CAN TAKE NO MORE!
NO, TUKTEE! YOU STILL HAVE YOUR LIFE!
IS THIS PITIFUL EXISTENCE SO MUCH TO LOSE? WE HAVE LOST OUR FAMILIES, OUR HOME-WORLD, OUR FREEDOM --WE HAVE NOTHING ELSE LEFT!
ALWAYS FIGURED I'D CATCH A BLASTER BOLT IN SOME COMBAT ZONE, NOT LIVE OUT MY YEARS ON THE WRONG END OF A WHIP.
WE'LL GET OUT OF HERE EVENTUALLY, CAPTAIN. MY CONCERN IS WHAT WILL BE LEFT OF THESE PEOPLE WHEN WE FINALLY DO.
ANAKIN WAS RIGHT, YOU CANNOT TRULY KNOW SLAVERY UNTIL YOU'VE EXPERIENCED IT.
I GUESS IT DOES CHANGE ONE FOREVER. THESE POOR SOULS HAVE LOST EVERYTHING.
AND EVERY TIME WE TRY TO HELP OR PROTECT THEM, THEY'RE PUNISHED FOR IT. BUT THE TRUTH IS WE HAVE ALREADY GIVEN SOMETHING BACK TO THEM! THEY JUST DON'T KNOW IT YET!

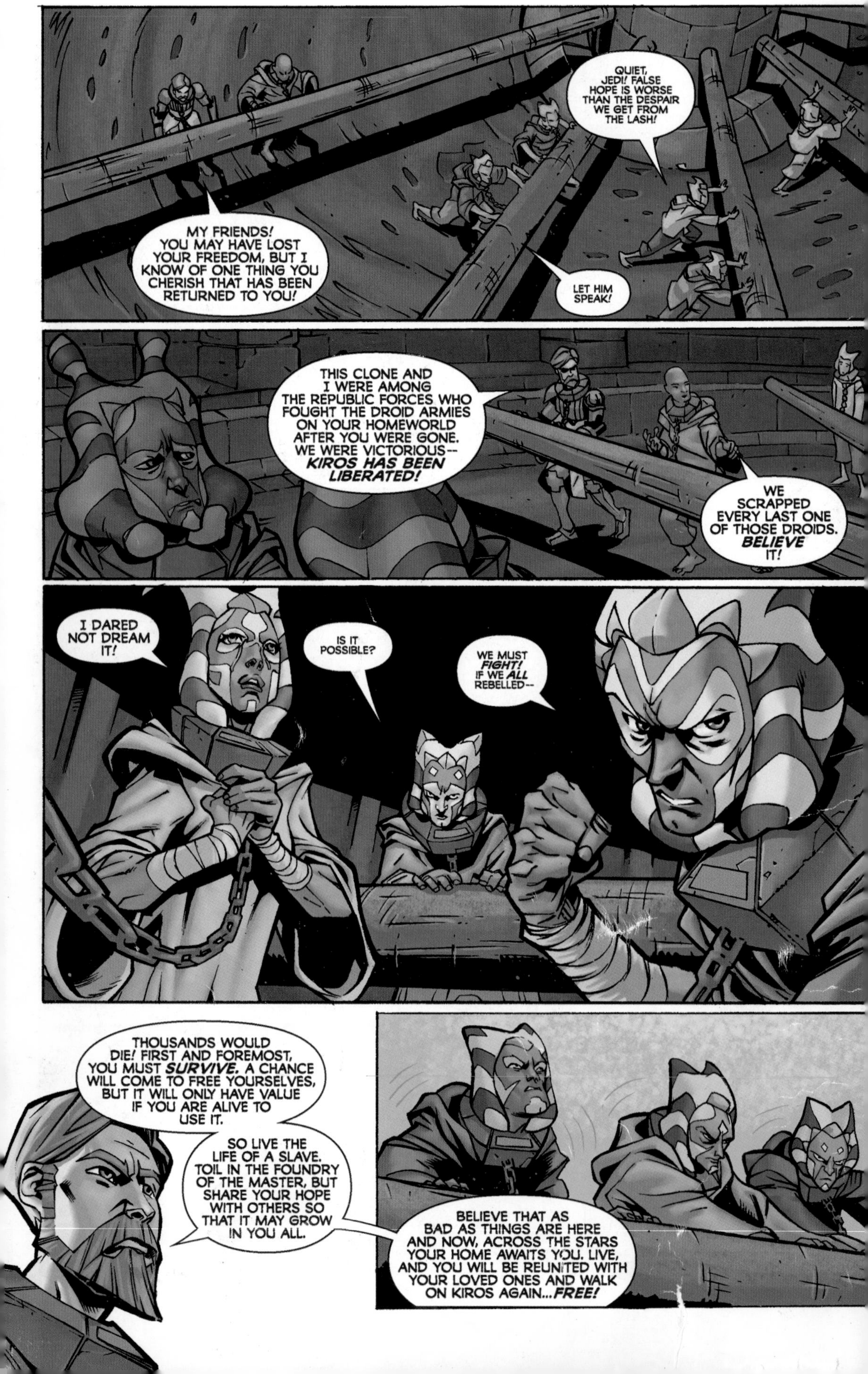
QUIET, JEDI! FALSE HOPE IS WORSE THAN THE DESPAIR WE GET FROM THE LASH!
MY FRIENDS! YOU MAY HAVE LOST YOUR FREEDOM, BUT I KNOW OF ONE THING YOU CHERISH THAT HAS BEEN RETURNED TO YOU!
LET HIM SPEAK!
THIS CLONE AND I WERE AMONG THE REPUBLIC FORCES WHO FOUGHT THE DROID ARMIES ON YOUR HOMEWORLD AFTER YOU WERE GONE. WE WERE VICTORIOUS-- KIROS HAS BEEN LIBERATED!
WE SCRAPPED EVERY LAST ONE OF THOSE DROIDS. BELIEVE IT!
I DARED NOT DREAM IT!
IS IT POSSIBLE?
WE MUST FIGHT! IF WE ALL REBELLED--
THOUSANDS WOULD DIE! FIRST AND FOREMOST, YOU MUST SURVIVE. A CHANCE WILL COME TO FREE YOURSELVES, BUT IT WILL ONLY HAVE VALUE IF YOU ARE ALIVE TO USE IT.
SO LIVE THE LIFE OF A SLAVE. TOIL IN THE FOUNDRY OF THE MASTER, BUT SHARE YOUR HOPE WITH OTHERS SO THAT IT MAY GROW IN YOU ALL.
BELIEVE THAT AS BAD AS THINGS ARE HERE AND NOW, ACROSS THE STARS YOUR HOME AWAITS YOU. LIVE, AND YOU WILL BE REUNITED WITH YOUR LOVED ONES AND WALK ON KIROS AGAIN...FREE!

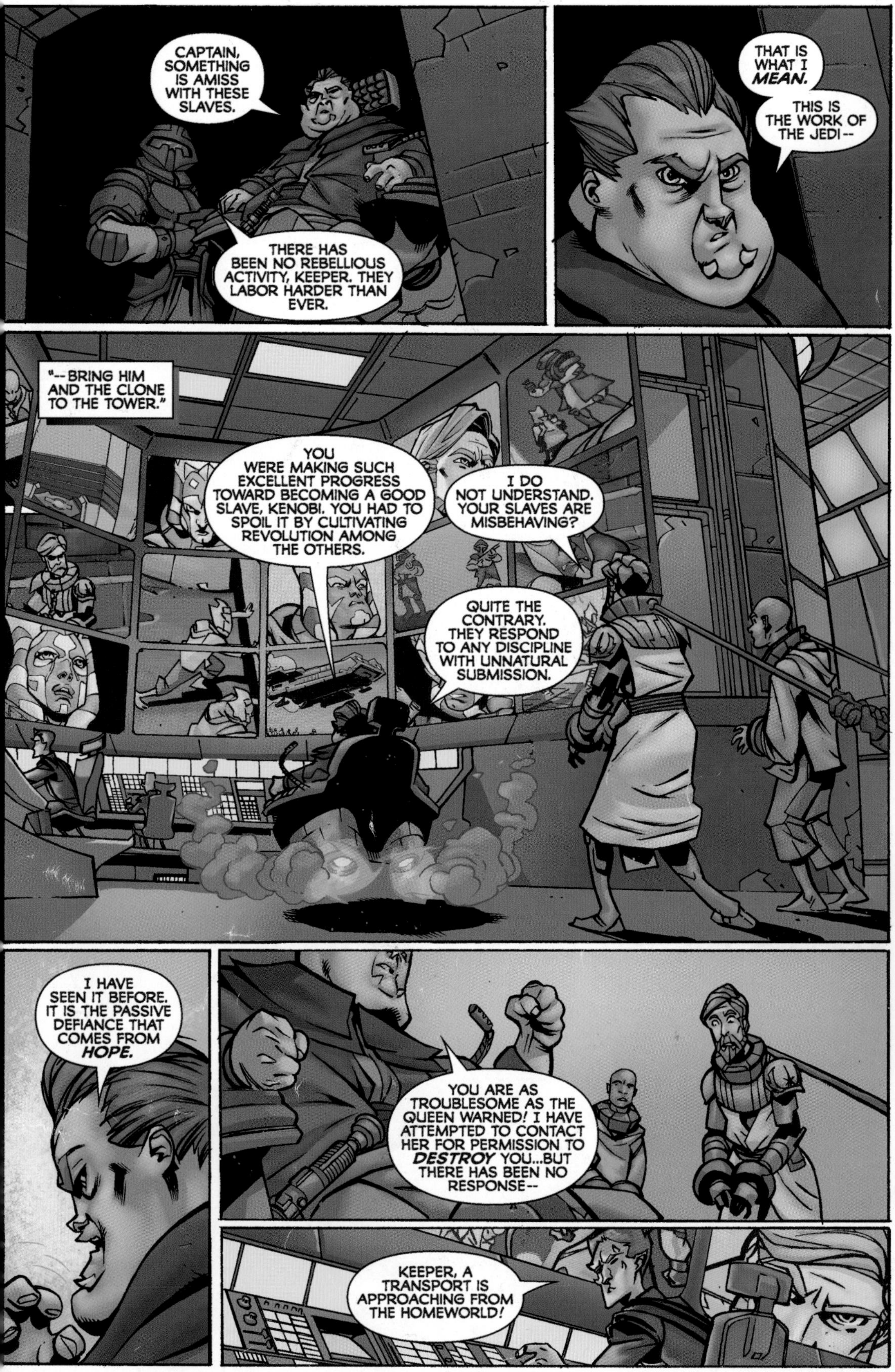
CAPTAIN, SOMETHING IS AMISS WITH THESE SLAVES.
THERE HAS BEEN NO REBELLIOUS ACTIVITY, KEEPER. THEY LABOR HARDER THAN EVER.
THAT IS WHAT I *MEAN.*
THIS IS THE WORK OF THE JEDI--
"--BRING HIM AND THE CLONE TO THE TOWER."
YOU WERE MAKING SUCH EXCELLENT PROGRESS TOWARD BECOMING A GOOD SLAVE, KENOBI. YOU HAD TO SPOIL IT BY CULTIVATING REVOLUTION AMONG THE OTHERS.
I DO NOT UNDERSTAND. YOUR SLAVES ARE MISBEHAVING?
QUITE THE CONTRARY. THEY RESPOND TO ANY DISCIPLINE WITH UNNATURAL SUBMISSION.
I HAVE SEEN IT BEFORE. IT IS THE PASSIVE DEFIANCE THAT COMES FROM *HOPE.*
YOU ARE AS TROUBLESOME AS THE QUEEN WARNED! I HAVE ATTEMPTED TO CONTACT HER FOR PERMISSION TO *DESTROY* YOU...BUT THERE HAS BEEN NO RESPONSE--
KEEPER, A TRANSPORT IS APPROACHING FROM THE HOMEWORLD!

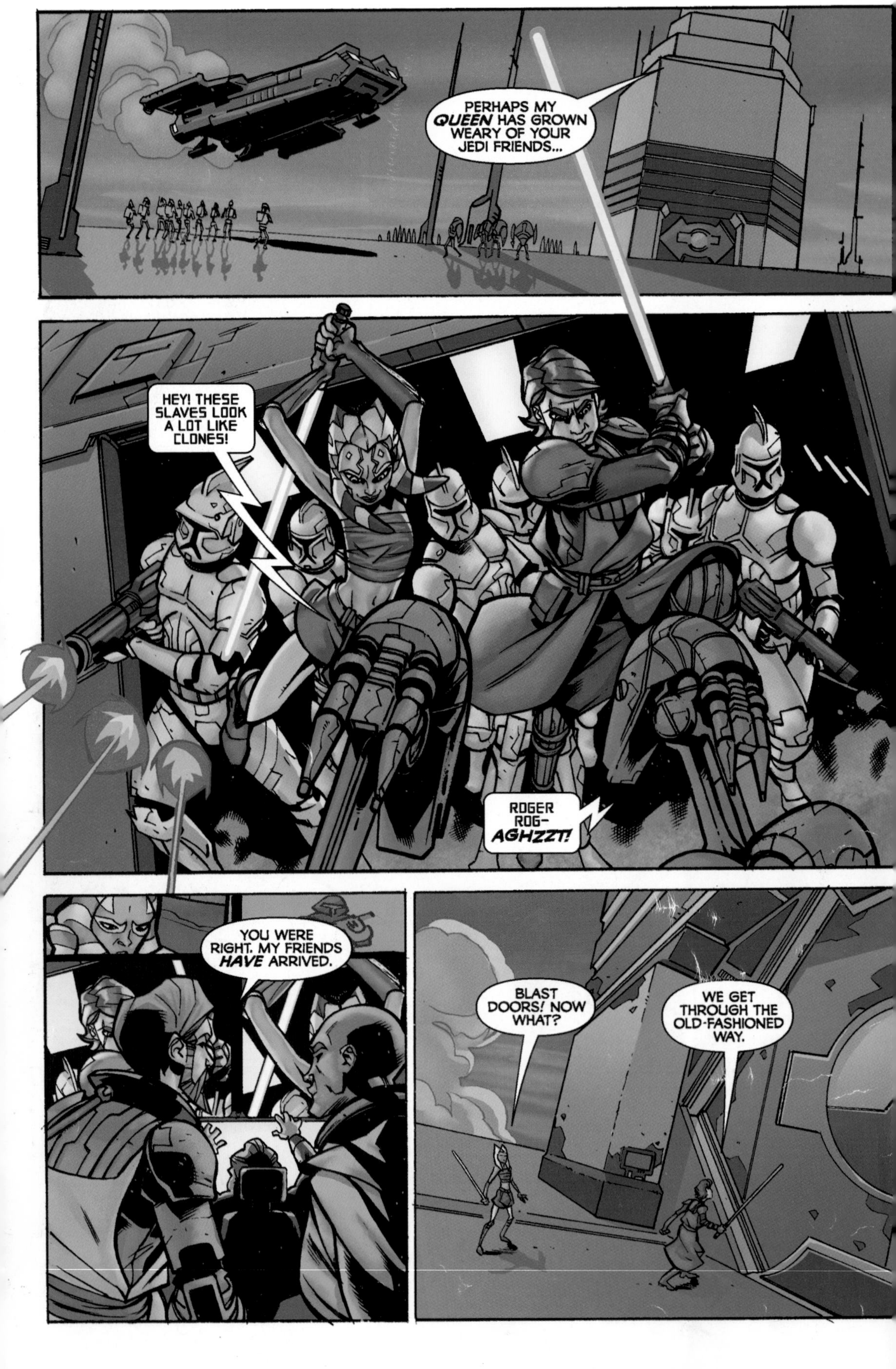
PERHAPS MY *QUEEN* HAS GROWN WEARY OF YOUR JEDI FRIENDS...
HEY! THESE SLAVES LOOK A LOT LIKE CLONES!
ROGER ROG- *AGHZZT!*
YOU WERE RIGHT. MY FRIENDS *HAVE* ARRIVED.
BLAST DOORS! NOW WHAT?
WE GET THROUGH THE OLD-FASHIONED WAY.

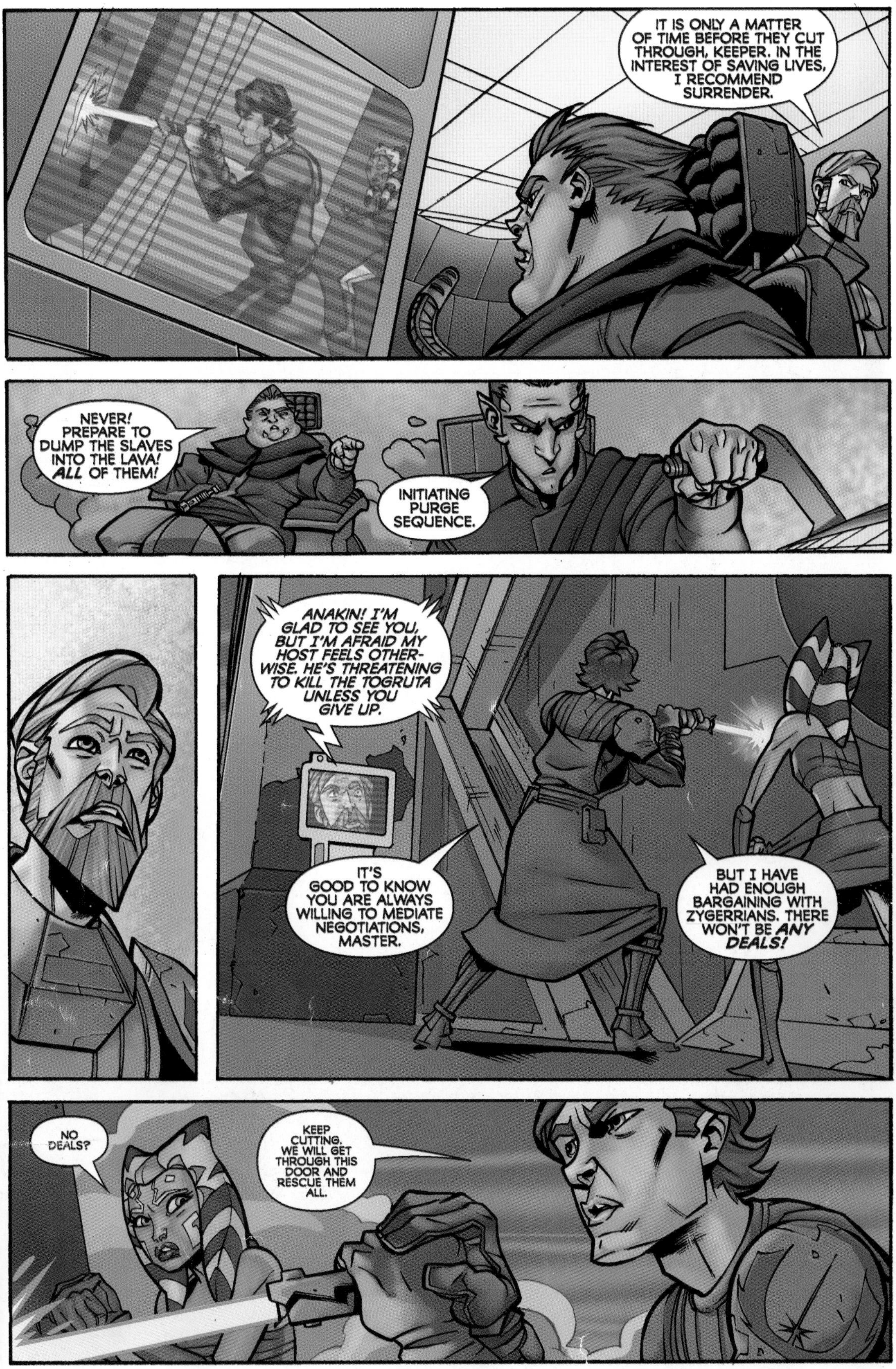
IT IS ONLY A MATTER OF TIME BEFORE THEY CUT THROUGH, KEEPER. IN THE INTEREST OF SAVING LIVES, I RECOMMEND SURRENDER.
NEVER! PREPARE TO DUMP THE SLAVES INTO THE LAVA! *ALL* OF THEM!
INITIATING PURGE SEQUENCE.
ANAKIN! I'M GLAD TO SEE YOU, BUT I'M AFRAID MY HOST FEELS OTHER-WISE. HE'S THREATENING TO KILL THE TOGRUTA UNLESS YOU GIVE UP.
IT'S GOOD TO KNOW YOU ARE ALWAYS WILLING TO MEDIATE NEGOTIATIONS, MASTER.
BUT I HAVE HAD ENOUGH BARGAINING WITH ZYGERRIANS. THERE WON'T BE *ANY DEALS!*
NO DEALS?
KEEP CUTTING. WE WILL GET THROUGH THIS DOOR AND RESCUE THEM ALL.

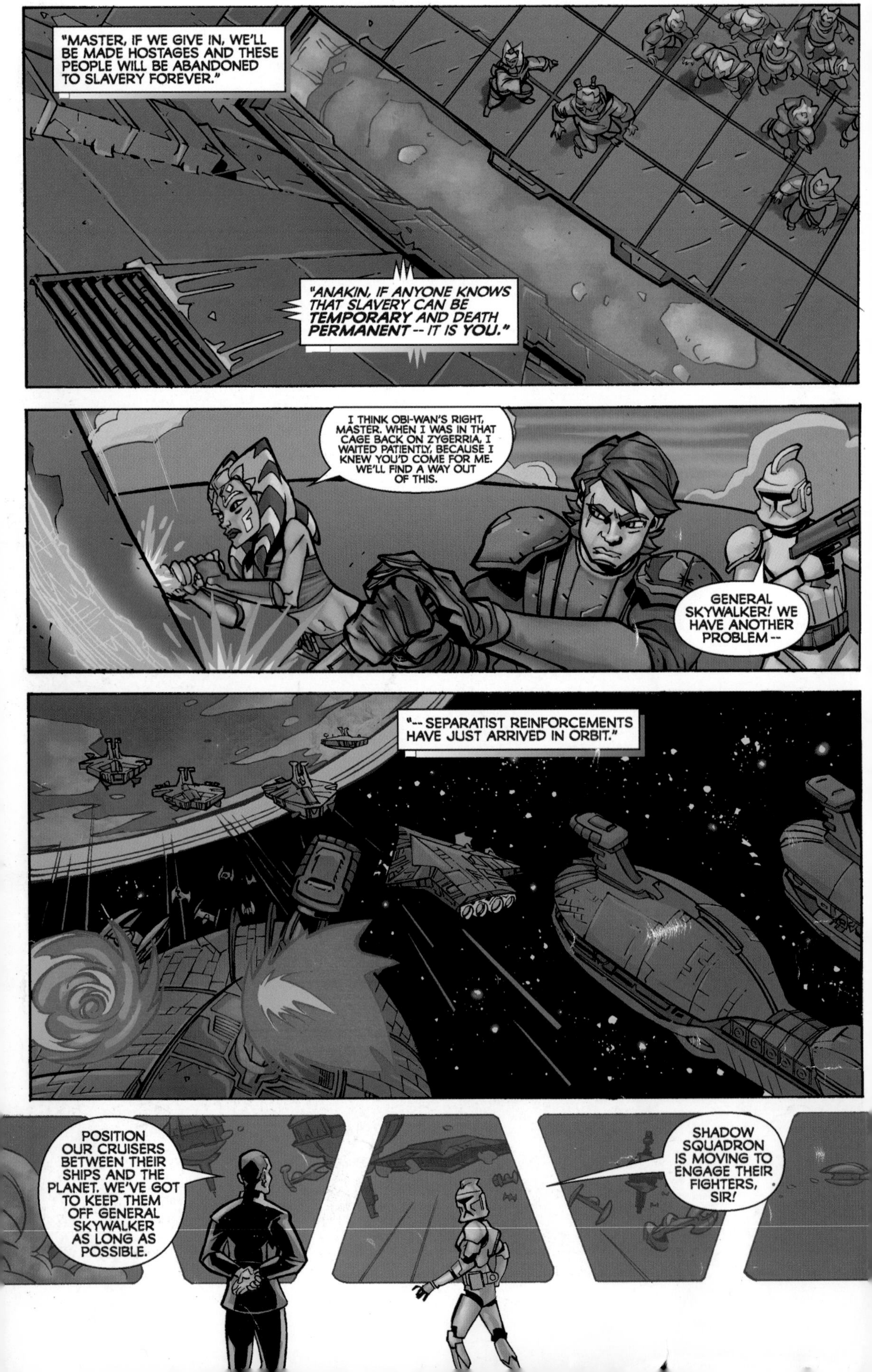
"MASTER, IF WE GIVE IN, WE'LL BE MADE HOSTAGES AND THESE PEOPLE WILL BE ABANDONED TO SLAVERY FOREVER."
"ANAKIN, IF ANYONE KNOWS THAT SLAVERY CAN BE TEMPORARY AND DEATH PERMANENT -- IT IS YOU."
I THINK OBI-WAN'S RIGHT, MASTER. WHEN I WAS IN THAT CAGE BACK ON ZYGERRIA, I WAITED PATIENTLY, BECAUSE I KNEW YOU'D COME FOR ME. WE'LL FIND A WAY OUT OF THIS.
GENERAL SKYWALKER! WE HAVE ANOTHER PROBLEM --
"-- SEPARATIST REINFORCEMENTS HAVE JUST ARRIVED IN ORBIT."
POSITION OUR CRUISERS BETWEEN THEIR SHIPS AND THE PLANET. WE'VE GOT TO KEEP THEM OFF GENERAL SKYWALKER AS LONG AS POSSIBLE.
SHADOW SQUADRON IS MOVING TO ENGAGE THEIR FIGHTERS, SIR!

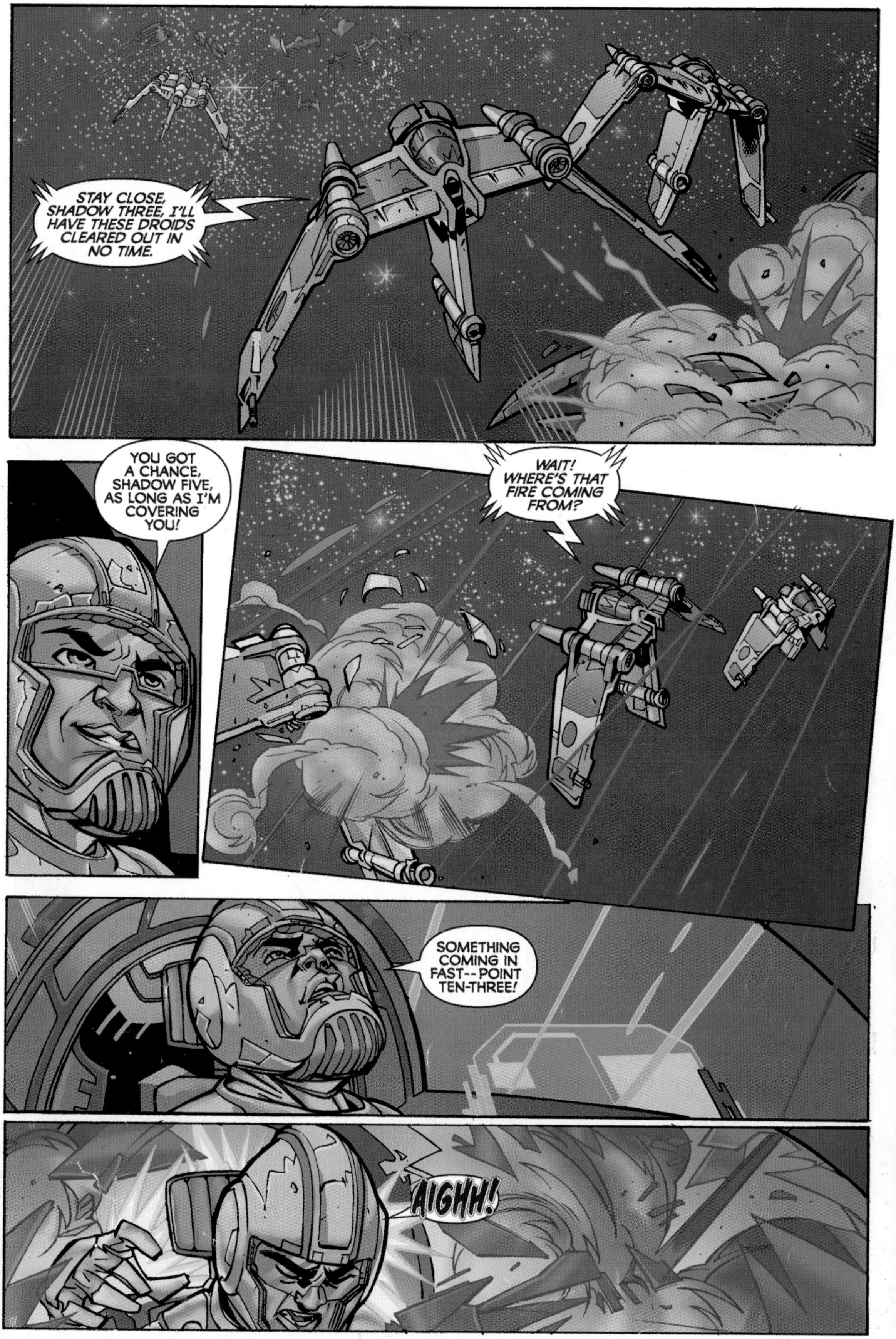
STAY CLOSE, SHADOW THREE, I'LL HAVE THESE DROIDS CLEARED OUT IN NO TIME.
YOU GOT A CHANCE, SHADOW FIVE, AS LONG AS I'M COVERING YOU!
WAIT! WHERE'S THAT FIRE COMING FROM?
SOMETHING COMING IN FAST--POINT TEN-THREE!
AIGHH!

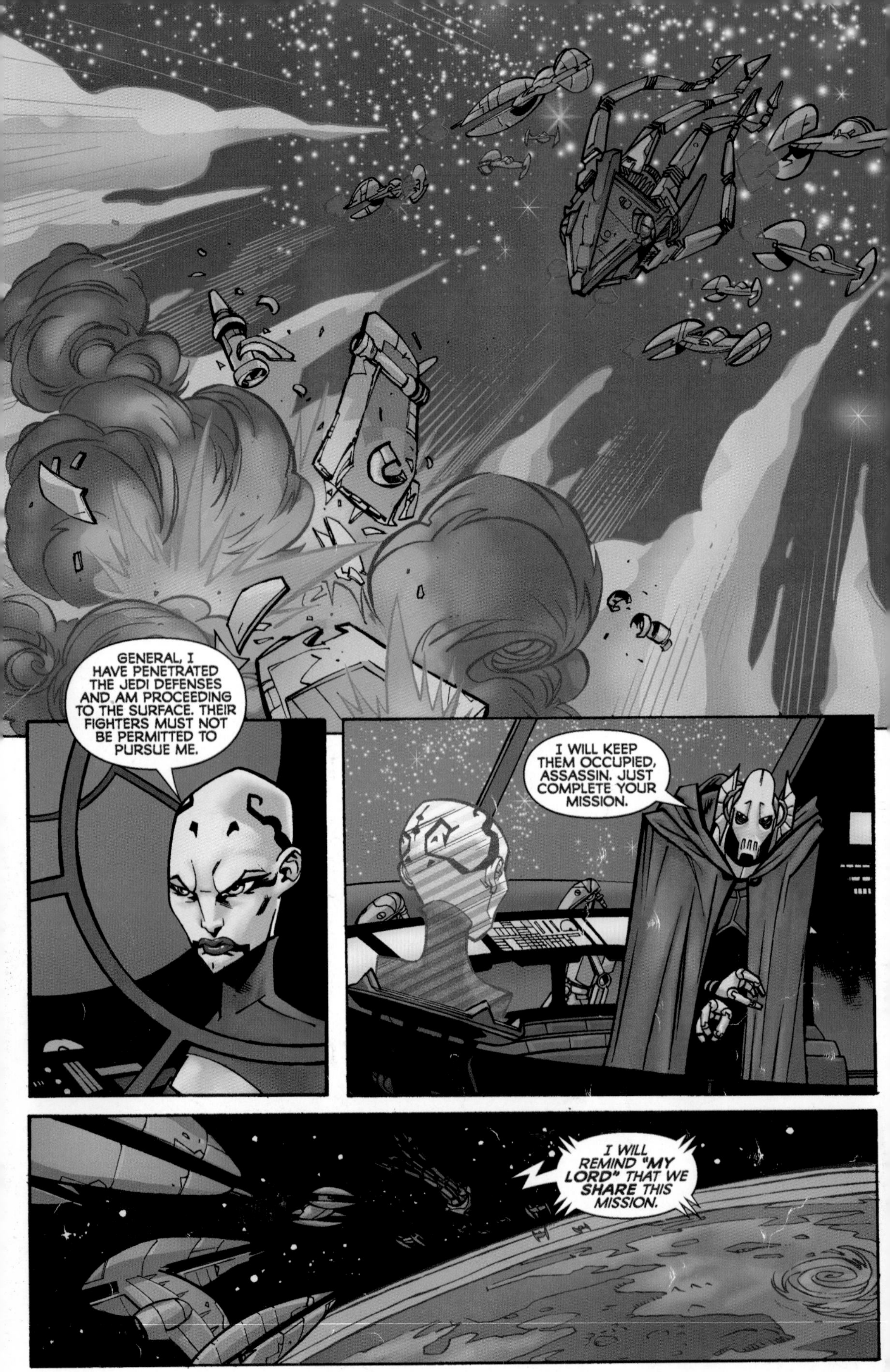
GENERAL, I HAVE PENETRATED THE JEDI DEFENSES AND AM PROCEEDING TO THE SURFACE. THEIR FIGHTERS MUST NOT BE PERMITTED TO PURSUE ME.
I WILL KEEP THEM OCCUPIED, ASSASSIN. JUST COMPLETE YOUR MISSION.
I WILL REMIND "MY LORD" THAT WE SHARE THIS MISSION.

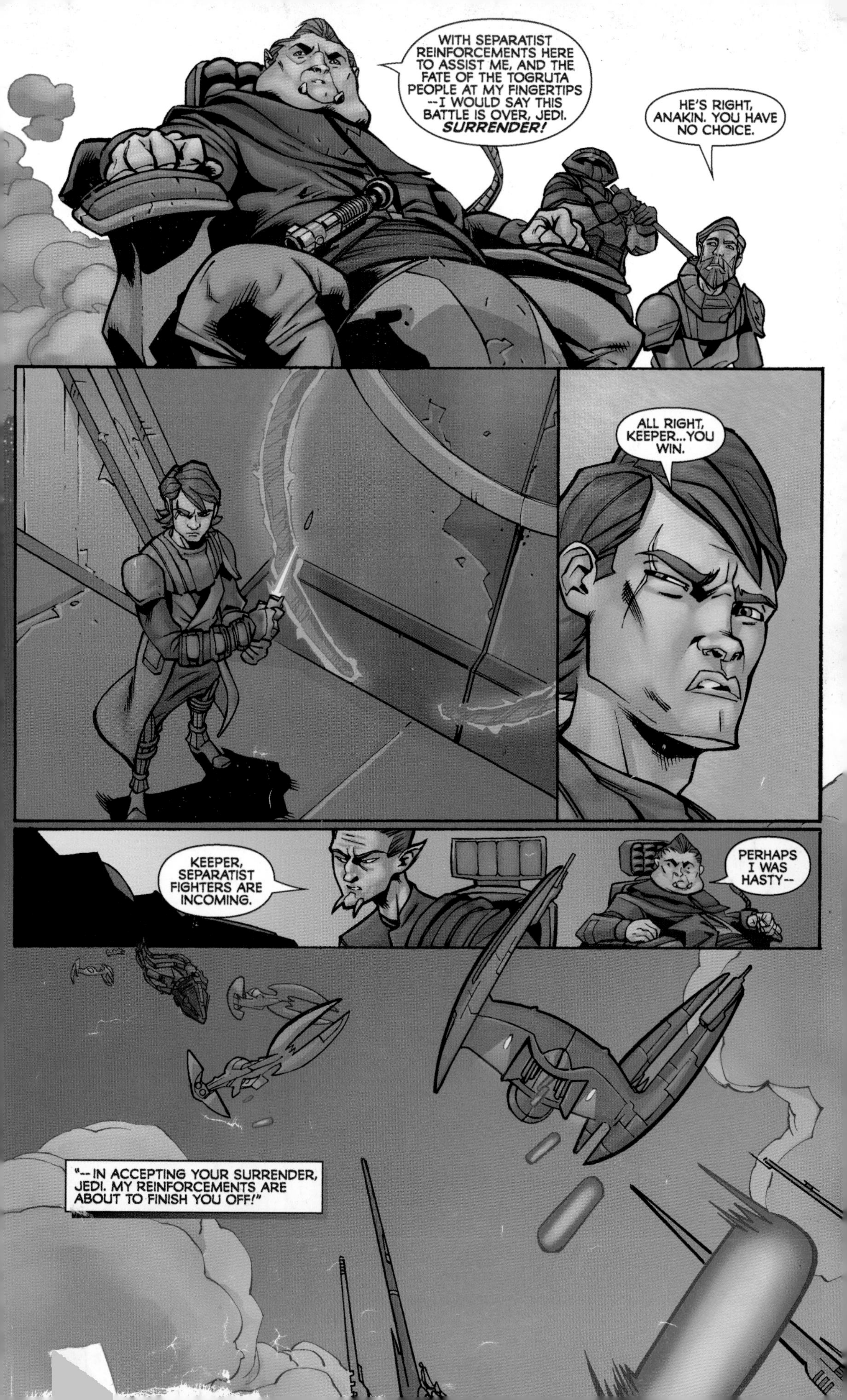
WITH SEPARATIST REINFORCEMENTS HERE TO ASSIST ME, AND THE FATE OF THE TOGRUTA PEOPLE AT MY FINGERTIPS --I WOULD SAY THIS BATTLE IS OVER, JEDI. SURRENDER!
HE'S RIGHT, ANAKIN. YOU HAVE NO CHOICE.
ALL RIGHT, KEEPER...YOU WIN.
KEEPER, SEPARATIST FIGHTERS ARE INCOMING.
PERHAPS I WAS HASTY--
"--IN ACCEPTING YOUR SURRENDER, JEDI. MY REINFORCEMENTS ARE ABOUT TO FINISH YOU OFF!"

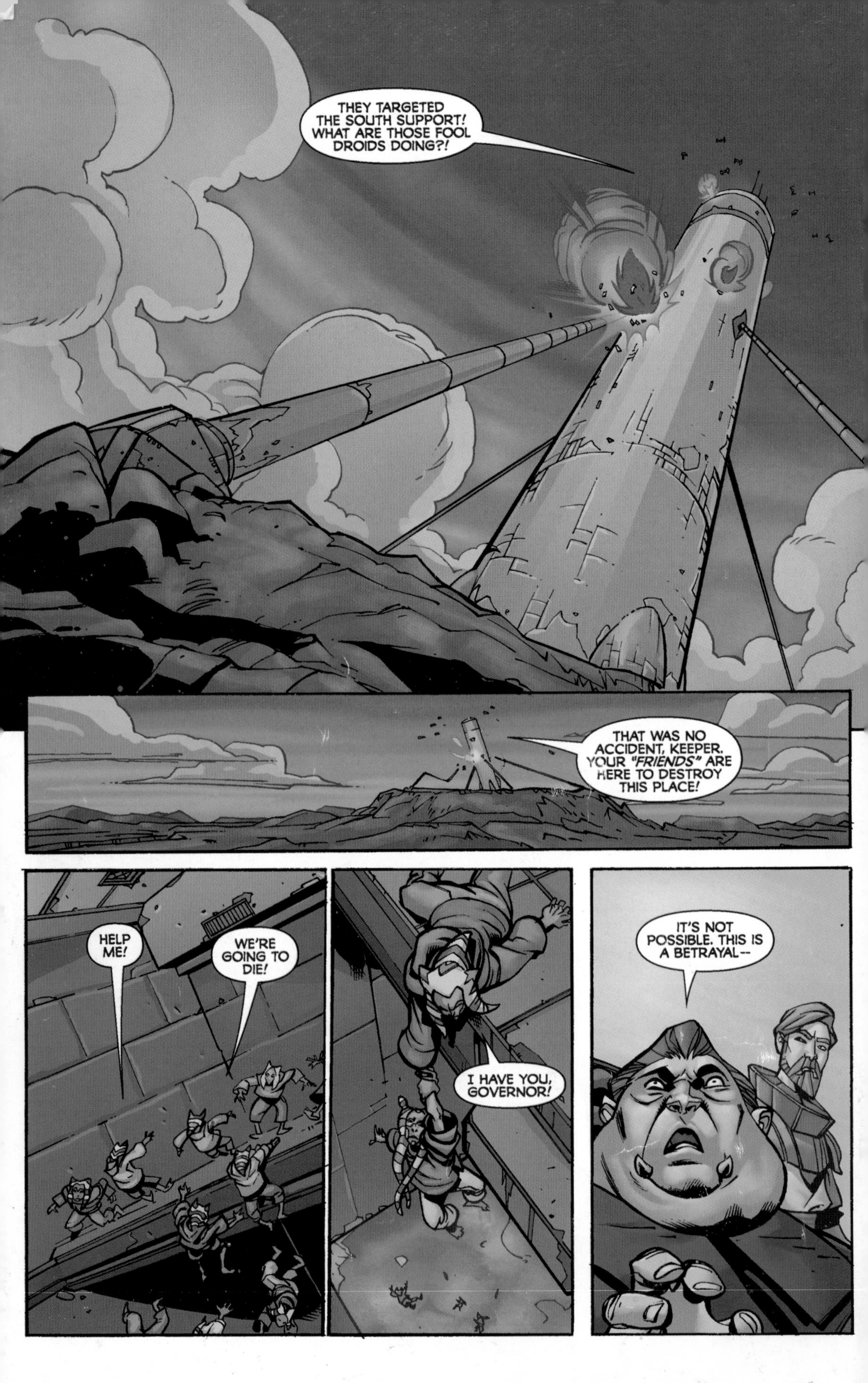

THEY TARGETED THE SOUTH SUPPORT! WHAT ARE THOSE FOOL DROIDS DOING?!
THAT WAS NO ACCIDENT, KEEPER. YOUR "FRIENDS" ARE HERE TO DESTROY THIS PLACE!
HELP ME!
WE'RE GOING TO DIE!
I HAVE YOU, GOVERNOR!
IT'S NOT POSSIBLE. THIS IS A BETRAYAL--

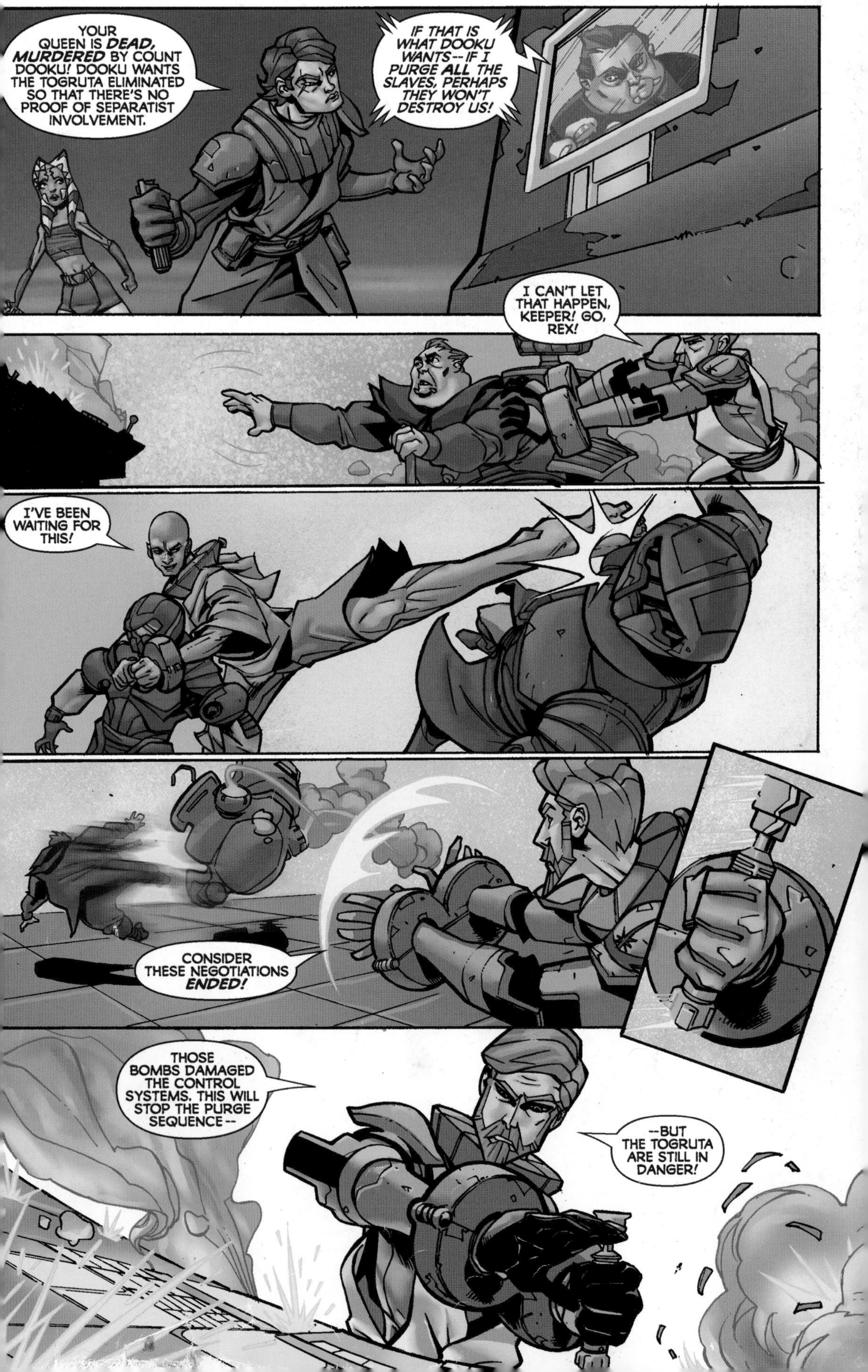
YOUR QUEEN IS DEAD, MURDERED BY COUNT DOOKU! DOOKU WANTS THE TOGRUTA ELIMINATED SO THAT THERE'S NO PROOF OF SEPARATIST INVOLVEMENT.
IF THAT IS WHAT DOOKU WANTS--IF I PURGE ALL THE SLAVES, PERHAPS THEY WON'T DESTROY US!
I CAN'T LET THAT HAPPEN, KEEPER! GO, REX!
I'VE BEEN WAITING FOR THIS!
CONSIDER THESE NEGOTIATIONS ENDED!
THOSE BOMBS DAMAGED THE CONTROL SYSTEMS. THIS WILL STOP THE PURGE SEQUENCE--
--BUT THE TOGRUTA ARE STILL IN DANGER!

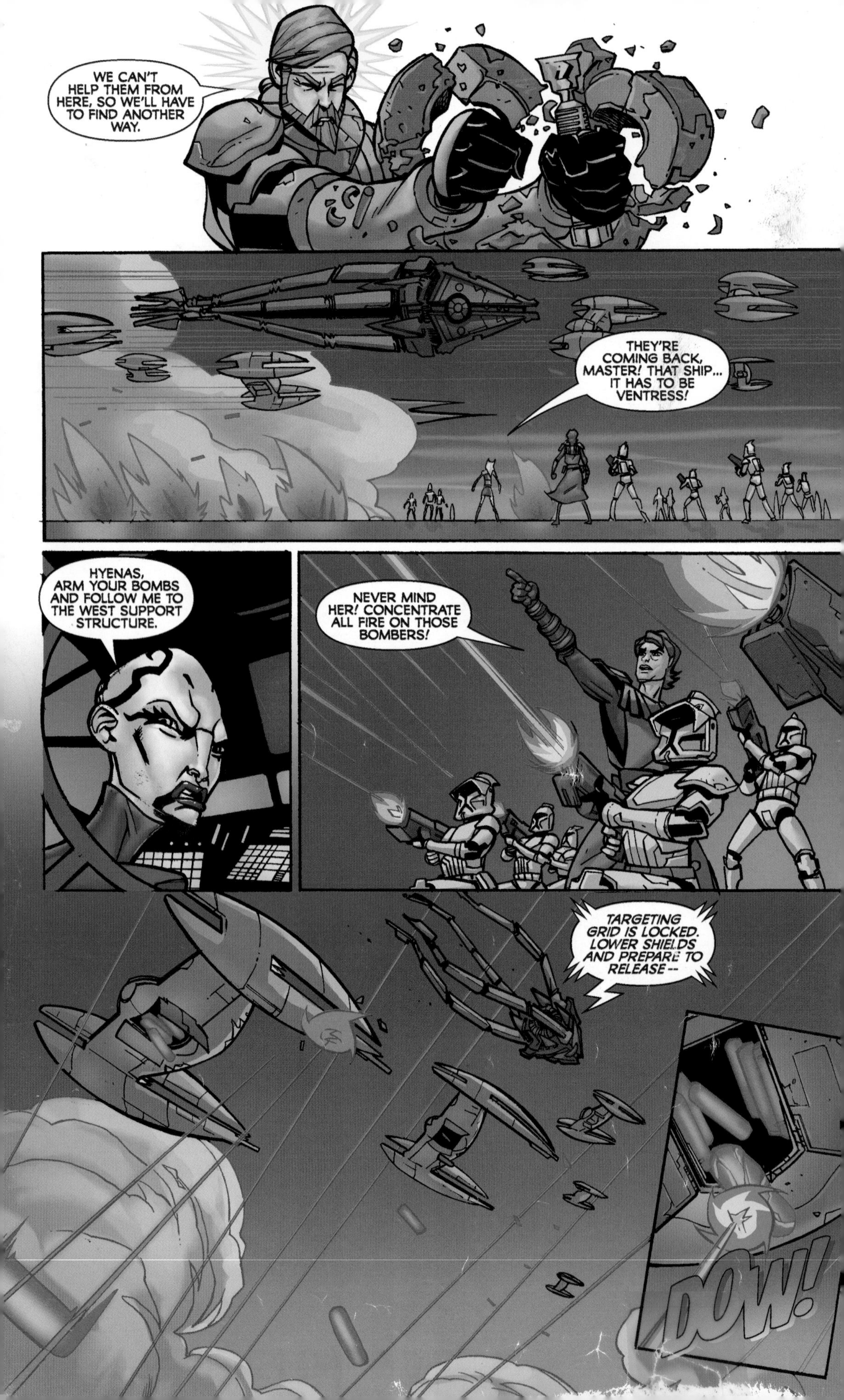
WE CAN'T HELP THEM FROM HERE, SO WE'LL HAVE TO FIND ANOTHER WAY.
THEY'RE COMING BACK, MASTER! THAT SHIP... IT HAS TO BE VENTRESS!
HYENAS, ARM YOUR BOMBS AND FOLLOW ME TO THE WEST SUPPORT STRUCTURE.
NEVER MIND HER! CONCENTRATE ALL FIRE ON THOSE BOMBERS!
TARGETING GRID IS LOCKED. LOWER SHIELDS AND PREPARE TO RELEASE --
DOW!

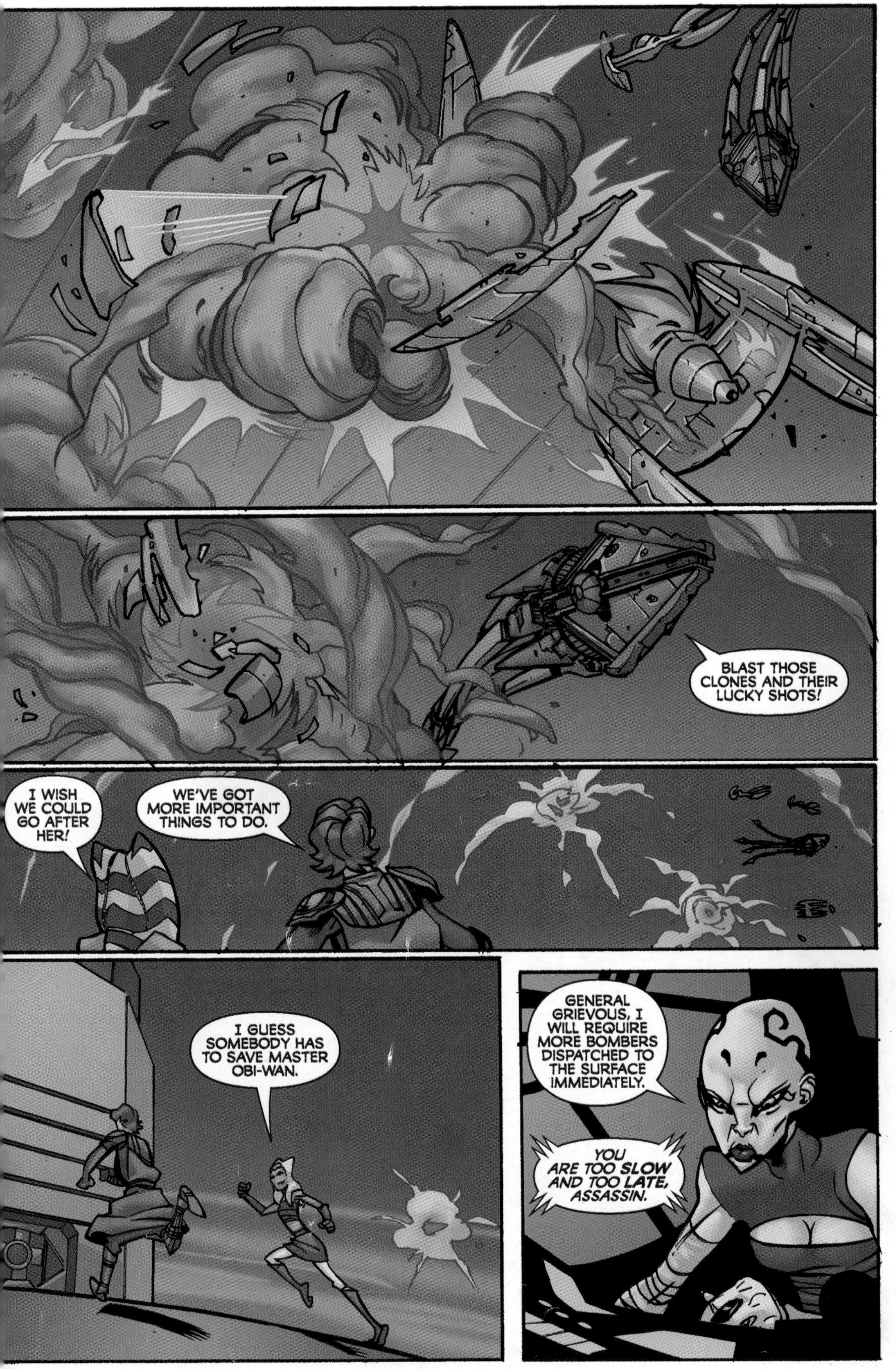
BLAST THOSE CLONES AND THEIR LUCKY SHOTS!
I WISH WE COULD GO AFTER HER!
WE'VE GOT MORE IMPORTANT THINGS TO DO.
I GUESS SOMEBODY HAS TO SAVE MASTER OBI-WAN.
GENERAL GRIEVOUS, I WILL REQUIRE MORE BOMBERS DISPATCHED TO THE SURFACE IMMEDIATELY.
YOU ARE TOO SLOW AND TOO LATE, ASSASSIN.

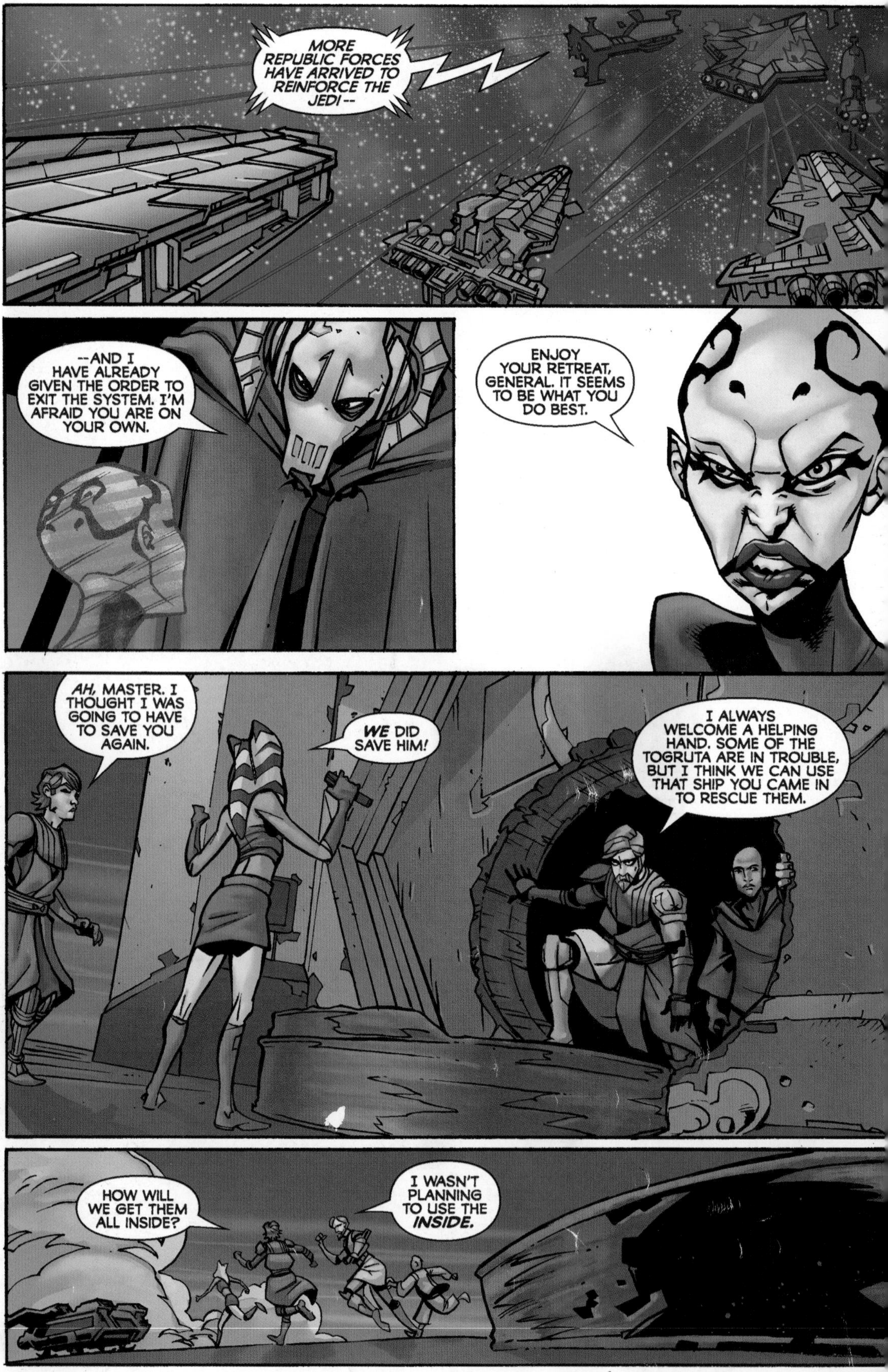
MORE REPUBLIC FORCES HAVE ARRIVED TO REINFORCE THE JEDI --
--AND I HAVE ALREADY GIVEN THE ORDER TO EXIT THE SYSTEM. I'M AFRAID YOU ARE ON YOUR OWN.
ENJOY YOUR RETREAT, GENERAL. IT SEEMS TO BE WHAT YOU DO BEST.
AH, MASTER. I THOUGHT I WAS GOING TO HAVE TO SAVE YOU AGAIN.
WE DID SAVE HIM!
I ALWAYS WELCOME A HELPING HAND. SOME OF THE TOGRUTA ARE IN TROUBLE, BUT I THINK WE CAN USE THAT SHIP YOU CAME IN TO RESCUE THEM.
HOW WILL WE GET THEM ALL INSIDE?
I WASN'T PLANNING TO USE THE ***INSIDE.***

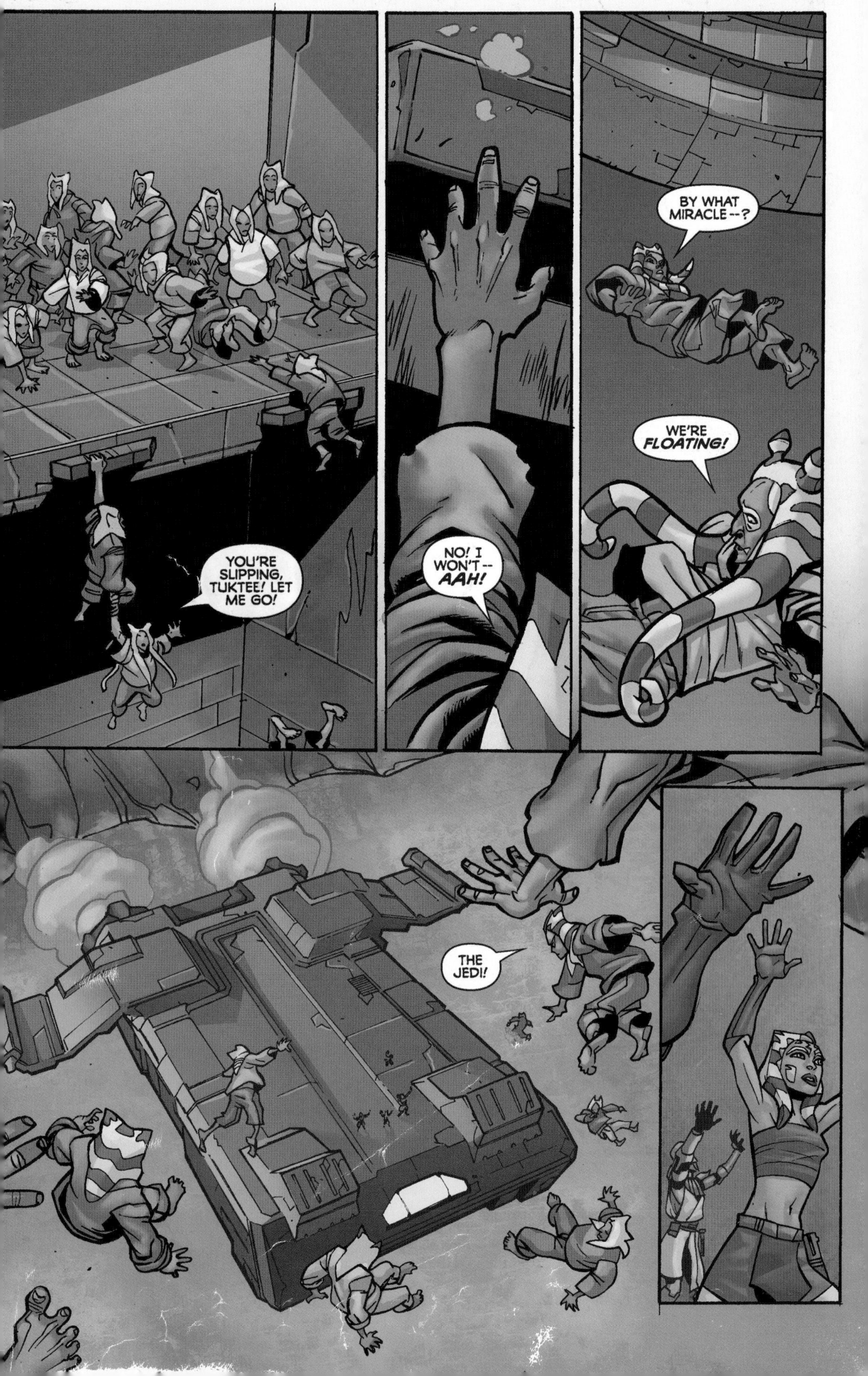
YOU'RE SLIPPING, TUKTEE! LET ME GO!
NO! I WON'T-- AAH!
BY WHAT MIRACLE--?
WE'RE FLOATING!
THE JEDI!

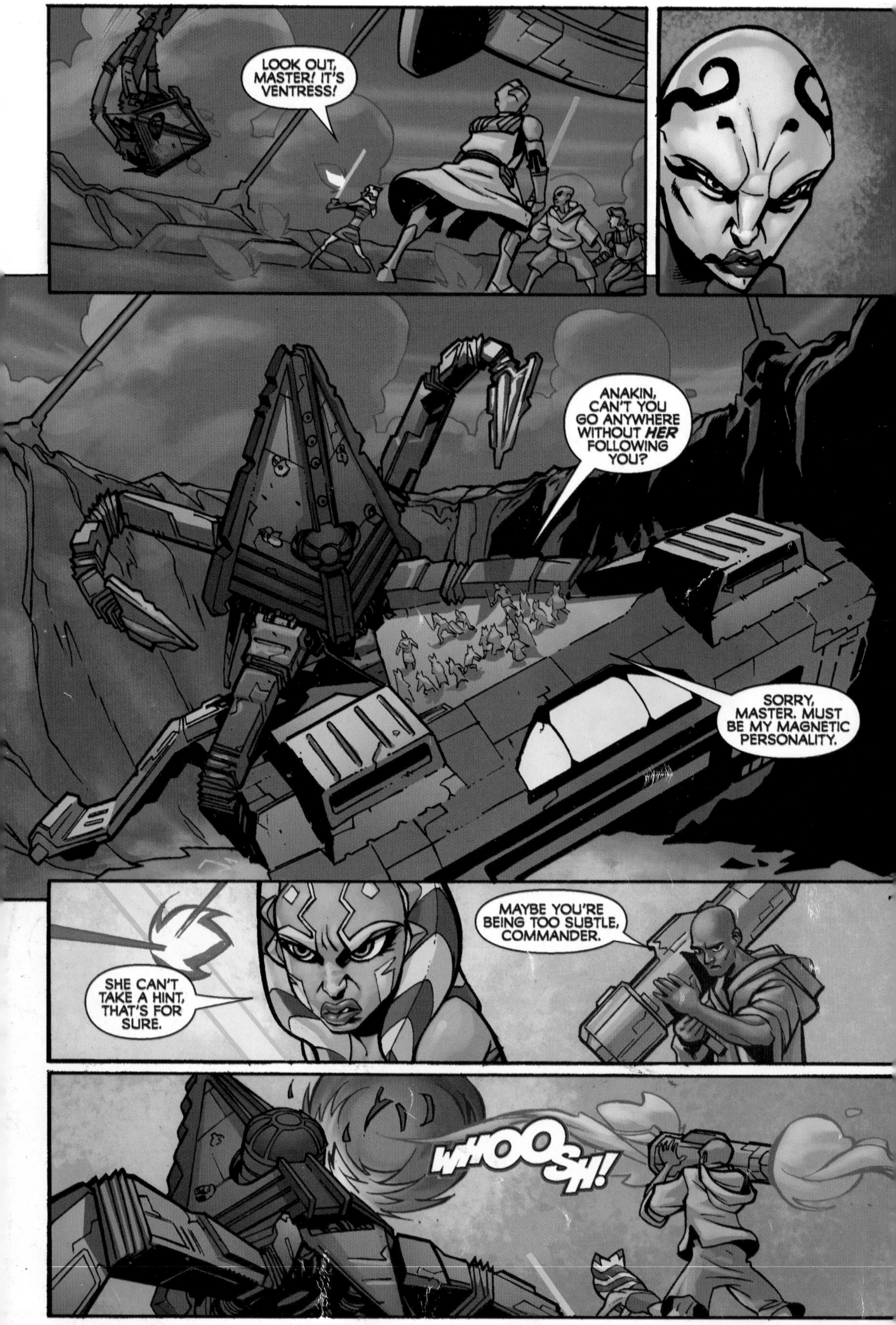
LOOK OUT, MASTER! IT'S VENTRESS!
ANAKIN, CAN'T YOU GO ANYWHERE WITHOUT *HER* FOLLOWING YOU?
SORRY, MASTER. MUST BE MY MAGNETIC PERSONALITY.
MAYBE YOU'RE BEING TOO SUBTLE, COMMANDER.
SHE CAN'T TAKE A HINT, THAT'S FOR SURE.
WHOOSH!

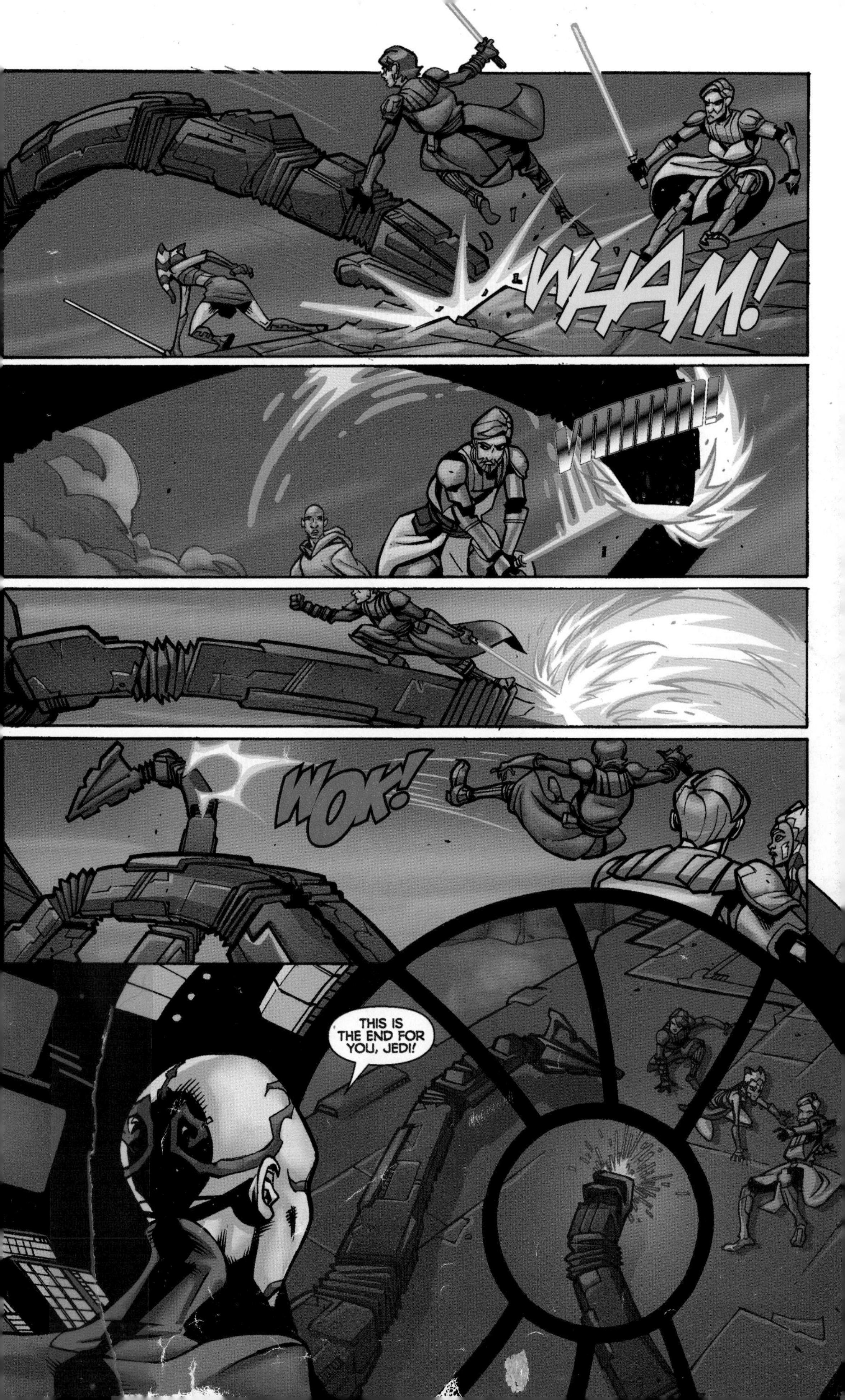
WHAM!
VMMMM!
WOK!
THIS IS THE END FOR YOU, JEDI!

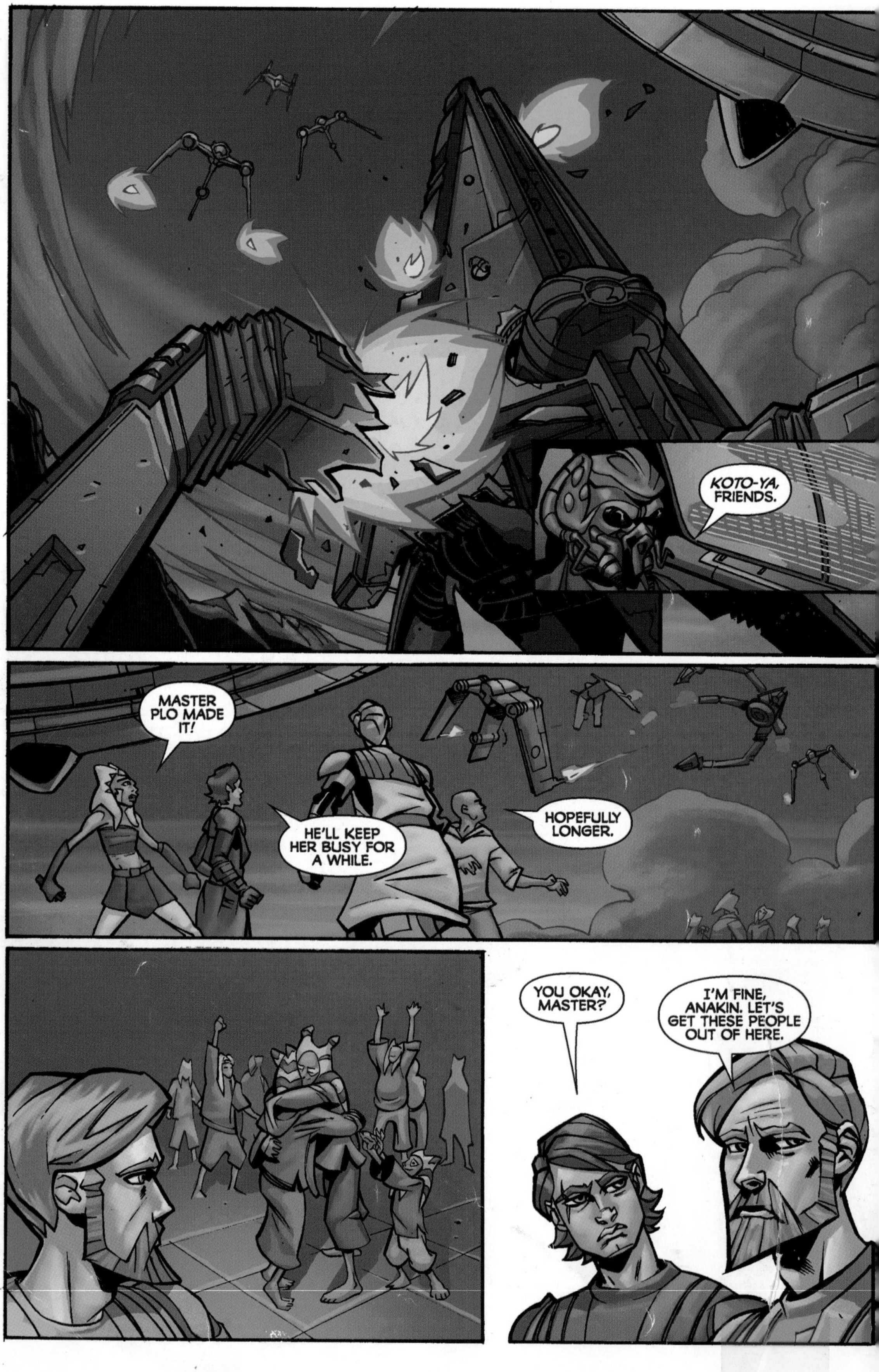
KOTO-YA, FRIENDS.
MASTER PLO MADE IT!
HE'LL KEEP HER BUSY FOR A WHILE.
HOPEFULLY LONGER.
YOU OKAY, MASTER?
I'M FINE, ANAKIN. LET'S GET THESE PEOPLE OUT OF HERE.

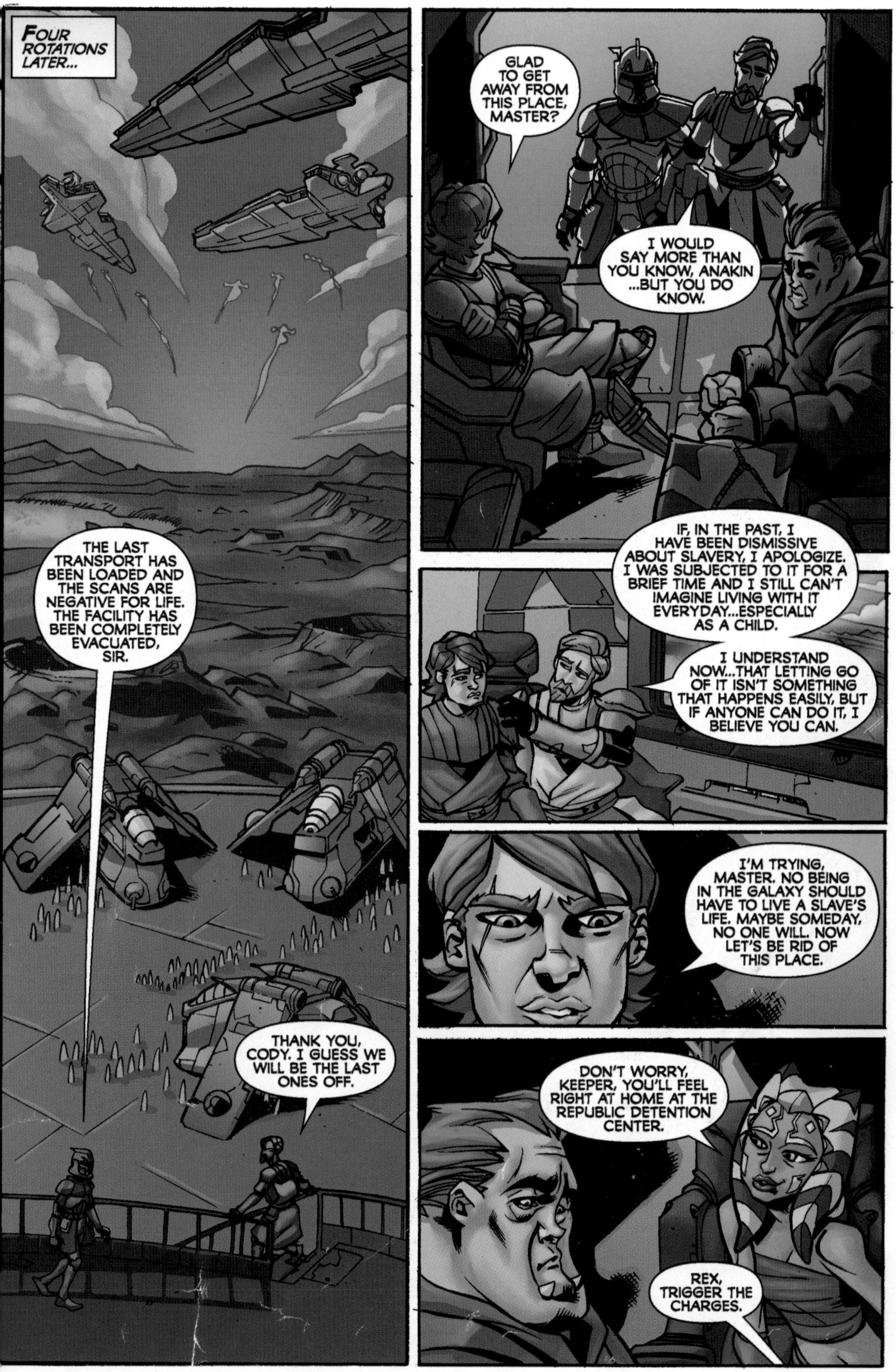
FOUR ROTATIONS LATER...
THE LAST TRANSPORT HAS BEEN LOADED AND THE SCANS ARE NEGATIVE FOR LIFE. THE FACILITY HAS BEEN COMPLETELY EVACUATED, SIR.
THANK YOU, CODY. I GUESS WE WILL BE THE LAST ONES OFF.
GLAD TO GET AWAY FROM THIS PLACE, MASTER?
I WOULD SAY MORE THAN YOU KNOW, ANAKIN ...BUT YOU DO KNOW.
IF, IN THE PAST, I HAVE BEEN DISMISSIVE ABOUT SLAVERY, I APOLOGIZE. I WAS SUBJECTED TO IT FOR A BRIEF TIME AND I STILL CAN'T IMAGINE LIVING WITH IT EVERYDAY...ESPECIALLY AS A CHILD.
I UNDERSTAND NOW...THAT LETTING GO OF IT ISN'T SOMETHING THAT HAPPENS EASILY, BUT IF ANYONE CAN DO IT, I BELIEVE YOU CAN.
I'M TRYING, MASTER. NO BEING IN THE GALAXY SHOULD HAVE TO LIVE A SLAVE'S LIFE. MAYBE SOMEDAY, NO ONE WILL. NOW LET'S BE RID OF THIS PLACE.
DON'T WORRY, KEEPER, YOU'LL FEEL RIGHT AT HOME AT THE REPUBLIC DETENTION CENTER.
REX, TRIGGER THE CHARGES.

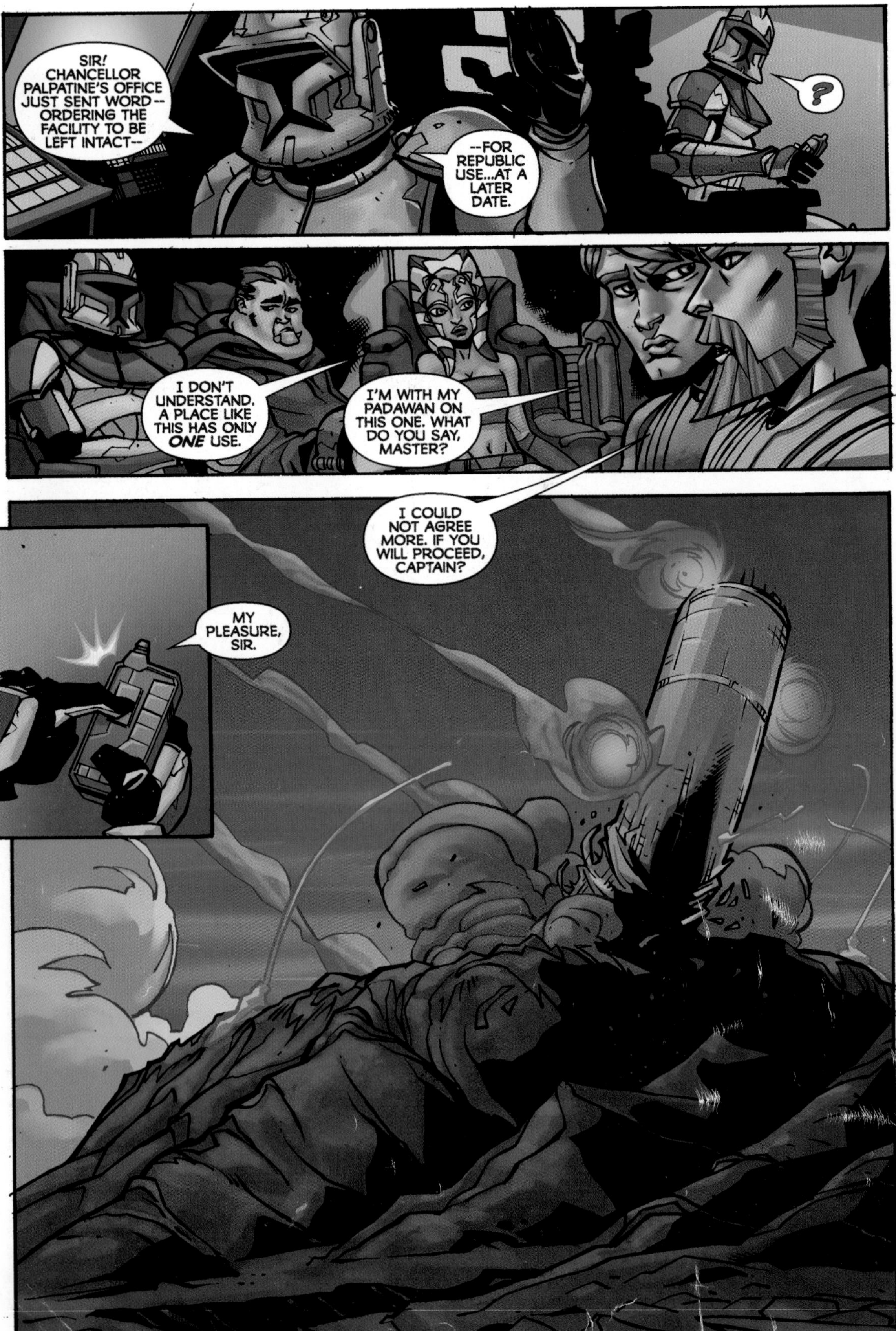
SIR! CHANCELLOR PALPATINE'S OFFICE JUST SENT WORD-- ORDERING THE FACILITY TO BE LEFT INTACT--
--FOR REPUBLIC USE...AT A LATER DATE.
?
I DON'T UNDERSTAND. A PLACE LIKE THIS HAS ONLY *ONE* USE.
I'M WITH MY PADAWAN ON THIS ONE. WHAT DO YOU SAY, MASTER?
I COULD NOT AGREE MORE. IF YOU WILL PROCEED, CAPTAIN?
MY PLEASURE, SIR.

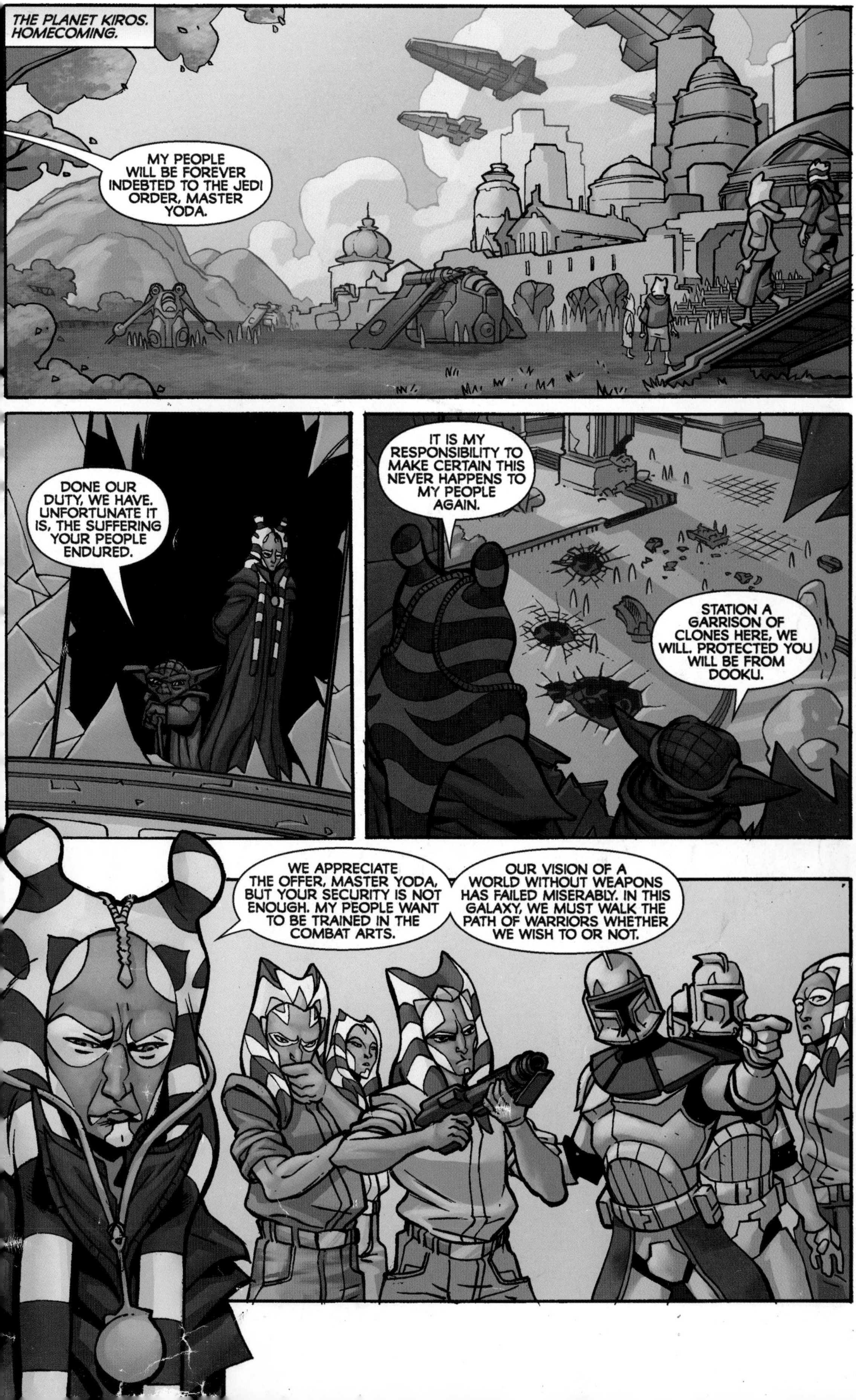
THE PLANET KIROS. HOMECOMING.
MY PEOPLE WILL BE FOREVER INDEBTED TO THE JEDI ORDER, MASTER YODA.
DONE OUR DUTY, WE HAVE. UNFORTUNATE IT IS, THE SUFFERING YOUR PEOPLE ENDURED.
IT IS MY RESPONSIBILITY TO MAKE CERTAIN THIS NEVER HAPPENS TO MY PEOPLE AGAIN.
STATION A GARRISON OF CLONES HERE, WE WILL. PROTECTED YOU WILL BE FROM DOOKU.
WE APPRECIATE THE OFFER, MASTER YODA, BUT YOUR SECURITY IS NOT ENOUGH. MY PEOPLE WANT TO BE TRAINED IN THE COMBAT ARTS.
OUR VISION OF A WORLD WITHOUT WEAPONS HAS FAILED MISERABLY. IN THIS GALAXY, WE MUST WALK THE PATH OF WARRIORS WHETHER WE WISH TO OR NOT.

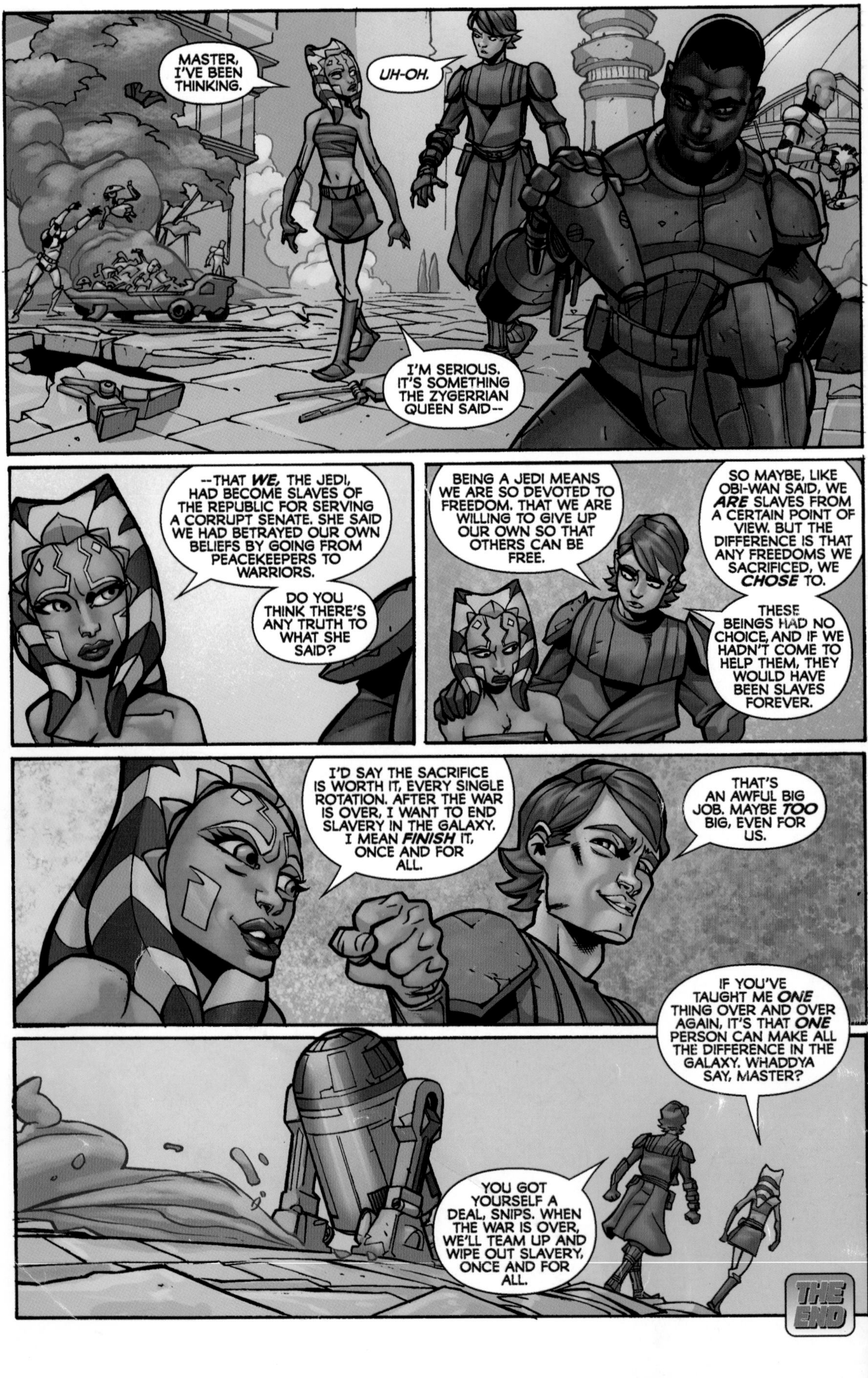

MASTER, I'VE BEEN THINKING.
UH-OH.
I'M SERIOUS. IT'S SOMETHING THE ZYGERRIAN QUEEN SAID--
--THAT *WE*, THE JEDI, HAD BECOME SLAVES OF THE REPUBLIC FOR SERVING A CORRUPT SENATE. SHE SAID WE HAD BETRAYED OUR OWN BELIEFS BY GOING FROM PEACEKEEPERS TO WARRIORS.
DO YOU THINK THERE'S ANY TRUTH TO WHAT SHE SAID?
BEING A JEDI MEANS WE ARE SO DEVOTED TO FREEDOM. THAT WE ARE WILLING TO GIVE UP OUR OWN SO THAT OTHERS CAN BE FREE.
SO MAYBE, LIKE OBI-WAN SAID, WE *ARE* SLAVES FROM A CERTAIN POINT OF VIEW. BUT THE DIFFERENCE IS THAT ANY FREEDOMS WE SACRIFICED, WE *CHOSE* TO.
THESE BEINGS HAD NO CHOICE, AND IF WE HADN'T COME TO HELP THEM, THEY WOULD HAVE BEEN SLAVES FOREVER.
I'D SAY THE SACRIFICE IS WORTH IT, EVERY SINGLE ROTATION. AFTER THE WAR IS OVER, I WANT TO END SLAVERY IN THE GALAXY. I MEAN *FINISH* IT, ONCE AND FOR ALL.
THAT'S AN AWFUL BIG JOB. MAYBE *TOO* BIG, EVEN FOR US.
IF YOU'VE TAUGHT ME *ONE* THING OVER AND OVER AGAIN, IT'S THAT *ONE* PERSON CAN MAKE ALL THE DIFFERENCE IN THE GALAXY. WHADDYA SAY, MASTER?
YOU GOT YOURSELF A DEAL, SNIPS. WHEN THE WAR IS OVER, WE'LL TEAM UP AND WIPE OUT SLAVERY, ONCE AND FOR ALL.
THE END